THE ART OF BEING A VAMPIRE

BY
KATE KARYUS QUINN

An imprint of Enslow Publishing

WEST **44** BOOKS™

Please visit our website, www.west44books.com.
For a free color catalog of all our high-quality books,
call toll free 1-800-398-2504.

Cataloging-in-Publication Data
Names: Quinn, Kate Karyus.
Title: The art of being a vampire / Kate Karyus Quinn.
Description: New York : West 44, 2024. | Series: West 44 YA verse
Identifiers: ISBN 9781978596719 (pbk.) | ISBN 9781978596702
(library bound) | ISBN 9781978596726 (ebook)
Subjects: LCSH: American poetry--21st century. | Poetry, Modern--
21st century.| Poetry.
Classification: LCC PPS584.Q419 2024 | DDC 811.008'09282--dc23

First Edition

Published in 2024 by
Enslow Publishing LLC
2544 Clinton Street
Buffalo, NY 14224

Editor: Caitie McAneney
Designer: Leslie Taylor

Photo Credits: Cover (girl) Jordan Whitfield/Unsplash.com, (trees)
Pat Tr/Shutterstock.com, (vampire) Subbotina Anna/Shutterstock.
com; Series Art (dripping blood) r2dpr/Shutterstock.com.

Printed in the United States of America

CPSIA compliance information: Batch #CS24W44: For further information contact
Enslow Publishing LLC, New York, New York at 1-800-398-2504.

To my amazing editor, Caitie—this
book wouldn't exist without you.

My Mama Was

what you
might call a
cautionary tale.

And a living
breathing
model
of the
         slippery
            s
              l
                o
                  p
                    e.

She was
the only
girl
in all of
Jerkins, Alabama,
to claim the
beauty queen
trifecta.

(That is,
winning
     all three
        Miss Pickle Crowns.
Little Miss Gerkin.
        Miss Teen Bread and Butter.
            Ms. Big Dill USA.)

She went from that
to ending her life
at 34 years
of age.
Dead
in a
dank apartment
with an
eviction notice
taped
to the
front door.

My Daddy,

most everyone
agrees,
was one of
the most
useless
      human
           beings
to walk the earth.

Grams said
Mama loved him
stupid.
Which is the
worst
kinda way
to love
anyone
     or
         anything.

She loved him
even after
he pulled
her under
with him.

Even after
he gave her
a baby
neither of 'em
wanted.

Then
left her
so's he could
run away
with a woman
who didn't yet
have the
two things
he'd given my mama.

Stretch scars
          and a
               drug habit
                    she couldn't kick.

Mama Didn't Love Me Stupid

Didn't love me smart neither.

There was
affection,
sure.

 Sloppy
        and
                trembling.

Mostly
I made her
feel bad.

Guilty for the
empty fridge.
The outgrown clothes.

Guilty for all
the times
I went to foster care.

Guilty for all
the times
she fell
back into her
old ways.

My Fate Seemed Sealed

Mama using
on one side,
and a
deadbeat dad
on the other.

Only Grams
gave me
hope.
Though not
too much of it.

"Likely,
blood will tell,
and you'll
go the same
way as
yer mother."

But with the help of
     Jesus our Lord
       and savior,
Grams said I could
be better than I was born to be.

She's Daddy's mama,
but she said,
"He ain't none
of mine now."

Grams said
bad blood
is like poison.

Better to
cut off
a sick limb—
        even her own son—
than risk
his weakness
spreading
to her.

Grams told me
I had to
do the same.
Or I'd end up

"a garbage person—
        just like
                the rest
                        of 'em."

When I
asked her
which part
of the Bible
that was from,
she answered
with narrowed
eyes.

"Don't get
smart
with me,
Shelby Ann."

I Never Did

find Jesus—
at least
not in Grams's church.

She mighta
pressed the issue
if she'd stuck around,
but she met Jim
while protesting
at a pride parade.

Not long after,
they married
and moved to
Arizona.

Grams's house
had been a place
to escape
Mama's chaos,
and also find a
hot cooked meal.

Without Grams,
I needed another
safe place.

The Next Year

I found my
new escape.
A photography class
at my
high school.

But it was
more than
just an escape.

Photography,
and
my camera,
was
something
to love.

And I
didn't
have to
worry
if it
loved
me
back.

It's a Dying Art

That's what
my teacher,
Mr. Bailey, said
about taking
photos on film.

According to
Mr. Bailey,
any dummy could
point and shoot
with a digital camera.

But without
autofocus
and
fancy
computer software
to fix screwups,
you had to
get it right.
Or else you'd
lose the shot.

I guess it was
lucky our school was
poor
and couldn't afford
nothing better
than what
we had.

"These old Nikons
are twenty years old,"
Mr. Bailey
would say,
holding up
one of the battered
camera bodies
we used in class.
"And they'll last
at least another
twenty—maybe more."

For me,
all that mattered
was being able to
hold it up
to my eye.
And with
the lens
between
me and
the world,
I could block out
all the
ugly
in my life.
I was
able to
be—
for at least
        a little bit—
something better
than what I was.

Life Is Funny

But not in a
HA HA
kinda way.

For example,
take the day
my whole world
changed.

I stayed after school
to use the darkroom
and develop some film.

As I hung the
dripping photos
to dry,
Mr. Bailey
came in to look.

The past weekend,
I'd taken my camera
and hopped on a bus
to an old church that
I'd read about online.

The light streamed through
tall windows
set high up
along the back wall.
I knew that I'd gotten
some really good shots.
But I wanted to hear
Mr. Bailey say it.

I guess I'd gotten
used to him
going on and on
about how talented
and special
I was.

But this time,
he saw my photo
with the
ribbon of light
making a statue glow
and he just said,

"It's pretty,
but I don't
feel anything.
Where's
          the
                    heart?"

I stood there,
shocked silent.

He told me my photos
never felt personal.
Like I was afraid
to put what I truly
felt, and who
I truly was,
on film.

Well, he was
          right
about that.

Taking photos
was my escape
from my real life.
I wanted to take
pictures that were
beautiful—
        <<<because>>>
                my life wasn't.

Of course,
I didn't say
none of that
to Mr. Bailey.
He wouldn't—
        couldn't—
possibly understand.

And then
as if
to prove
my point,
I went home
and found
my Mama's
dead body.

Poor Mama

She must have
lain dead
for hours
before I
made it home
and found her.

I was glad
at least
she was
in bed.

I almost coulda
pretended she
was sleeping
or passed out.
Those things
weren't unusual.

But she was
still and silent.
Eyes blank.

When I'd left
for school
that morning,
she'd been
awake
and pacing.

Waiting for
Apollo
(her current squeeze,
          though more like sleaze)
to come with
drugs like
he'd promised.

I guess
he showed up
eventually.

I Called 911

The operator
made me check
for a pulse.
Just to make sure
she was dead.

For a second
it got me
            hoping.
Maybe I was wrong.
I was just a kid,
not a doctor.

But the moment
my fingers
touched Mama's
cold skin,
I knew
there weren't no
blood beating
beneath it.
            Not anymore.

I hung up.
Reached for
my camera
from school.
I just wanted
to feel it in
my hands.

The same way
I'd squeezed
a stuffed bunny
when I was little.

But the usual
comfort wasn't there.
Mr. Bailey's
words still
echoed inside
my head.

I wanted
to pull him
into this room.
Rub his nose
in this scene.

See? I'd say.
Does this
look like
        art?

Mama.
        Mama.

I wanted to
rage at her,
but she was
gone—
        for good this time.

Somehow that
seemed like
Mr. Bailey's
fault, too.

Him and
everyone
else who
didn't understand.
Who
didn't see.
Who let this
happen
to Mama . . .
        and me.

I guess
my thoughts
weren't
        quite
                right
in my head.
Cause
I decided
that I would
show
Mr. Bailey.
I would
        show
                everyone.
He wanted
something
        real and raw?
He wanted
        heart?

Well here it was.
I'd tear free
a chunk of mine.

I Lifted the Camera

But instead
of focusing
on Mama,
I pointed it at
the big ugly
oil painting
portrait
over her bed.

It was part
of her prize
when she won
Miss Teen Bread and Butter.

In the painting, she's
impossibly
young and
beautiful.
Her hair
defying gravity.
Topped
with a
glittering crown.
Her smile
is so easy.

The young woman
in that painting
has no idea
what's to come.

In the next year,
she'd meet my
daddy.
Then all the
trouble would begin.

But in that moment,
she's innocent.
And hopeful.
And totally
clueless
about how
bad things
will get.

Getting down
on the floor,
I was able to
put Mama,
dead and cold,
in the foreground.
I left her
dead body
fuzzy and blurred
while placing
the portrait
in crystal clear
focus.
It looked like
Mama's
younger self
was looking down
on what she'd
become.

I went through
a whole roll
of film.
Adjusting
the lights
and angles.
Lost in the work.

Then there was
a knock at the door,
and I realized
someone had finally
come to take
Mama away.

I Never

showed those
photos to
Mr. Bailey.

I developed
the film
the next day.
Going to school
like nothing
had changed.
Like Mama
was still
alive.

Normally,
I loved the magic
of watching
a photo appear
in the pan
full of chemicals.
But this time,
            I
        looked
            away.
People always
said
that my
soft curls
and
sweet smile
made me
look the spittin' image
of Mama.

I'd never seen it.
But there
in the
darkroom,
I felt like it was
my own face
coming into being.
My own fate.

I always
named my
photos.
It made me
feel fancy.
This one
I called
Fear the Future.

Cause Mama didn't,
       but I do.

I wrote the name
on a manilla folder.
Then slipped the
barely dried
photo inside.

Eventually,
it got packed away
in the same box
that held Mama's ashes.

Nobody Wanted Me

That's been the story
of my life.
Mama's death
sure didn't
change that.

Grams couldn't
take me
cause of Jim's
health.
My daddy
moved around
so much,
nobody even
bothered to keep
track no more.

Eventually,
an Aunt Clara
I'd never even
heard of
before
came forward.

She's daddy's sister,
but Grams
never once
spoke her name.

Turns out,
Grams kicked
Aunt Clara
outta her house at 16
for kissing a girl.

You'd think
Aunt Clara
wouldn't care
to take in
the child
of the family
that threw her
away.

But I guess
despite having
Grams for a
mother,
she somehow
came to believe in
        mercy
            and
                forgiveness.

Anyway, that's
how I ended up
in a fancy
southern suburb
living with a
stranger.

My Aunt Was a Lot

The first time
we met,
she talked at me
for a solid
10 minutes.
Telling me:

what to call her
        (Just Clara is fine.
        Though Aunt Clara
        was okay too.)

what she does
        (She's something called a
        "data analyst."
        She seemed to mostly
        sit at a computer and
        make a lot of money.)

and that I'll
be attending
a private school
down the road.
        (A place called
        St. Bartholomew's.)

Those are just
the highlights.

Then she started
to quiz me.
What did I like to eat?

How would I like
to set up my room?
Did I need clothes?
Bras or underwear? (OMG!)
Could I make her
a list of my
favorite brands
of soap, toothpaste, etc. (Favorite brand!?)

She reminded me
a bit of Grams
with her
intensity.

It was all too much.

That first day,
I yelled at her
that I didn't care
and didn't plan
on being there
that long.

That pretty much
set the tone
for things between us.

She'd Tried So Hard

Wanting to talk.
Wanting to find someone
for me to "talk to."
     (She meant a shrink.)

She even
saw my old camera
from school.
     (I'd "forgotten"
     to return it.)
And the very
next day,
she came home
with this fancy
new one.

Digital, of course.

With a sneer,
I pushed it away.
Refused to even
open the box.

It was a beautiful camera.
Way nicer
than anything
I'd even come
close to.
I don't know why
I hated it so much.
But I did.

I wanted to
smash it
to pieces.
I wanted to
smash everything
and everyone.

Especially
Aunt Clara.

And the more
she pushed,
the more
I hated her.

It was
so obvious
I didn't
            fit
in her
perfect life.

I knew
she'd
eventually
figure it out,
too.

School Was Even Worse

I usually kept to myself.
But my first week—
        I punched a girl
right in the face.
Almost
got myself
kicked out
of that fancy,
        uptight
                school.

But Clara came in
and told 'em
the sad story
of my dead mama.
So they gave
me a second chance.
Acting like
it was a real act
of charity.

So glad
I could be
their good deed
for the day.

And not just that,
but also a
learning moment
for the mean girl
who'd asked me

if I'd meant to
dress like a
"cheap prostitute."
Because us girls
needed to stick
together
and lift
each other
up.

Pfft. Whatever.
It wasn't what
she'd said—
not really.

It was more like
I'd been wanting
to punch
something.
Anything.

I guess
you could say
I was mad.

After 16 years
of always getting
the short end
of the stick,
I'd had enough.

I wasn't
gonna be
following
the rules
or staying on
the straight
and narrow.

Not anymore.

I was sick
of clinging to
the slippery slope.

What had
        being good
                ever gotten me?

I Met Brandt

my second week
at St. Bart's.

He came to
my lunch
table.
Sat across
from me
and asked,

"Is it true?
You gave
Charity Wilkes
a black eye?"

I shrugged.
Playing
at being
cool.
"Yeah, so?"

He grinned
at me then.

"Thank god
somebody
interesting
has finally
arrived
at this
school,"
he said.

My heart
flip-flopped
in my chest.
From his
smile.
From his
words.
From . . .
          him.

See, Brandt
had this
mysterious
          sorta
                    way
about him.

First off,
he was gorgeous.
But he was also moody.
Had a sulky mouth
like a character
from a movie
where he gets the girl
even though the other guy
was nicer and prettier and richer.
Because she wants
the bad boy.
The one with
floppy hair
that covers one eye.
And they end up
outside
          kissing
                    in the pouring
                              rain.

I wanted
to kiss him
in the pouring
rain.

Right there.
Right then.

I guess that was
my first introduction
to wanting something
bad enough
to not care
about the
consequences.

The Next Day

Brandt asked me
to skip school
with him.

I did.

We hung out
all afternoon.
Just walking
around town.
Talking about
how much
everyone
and
everything
          sucked.

By our
accounting,
it was
          A LOT.

We laughed
too.

Something
I hadn't
done much of
lately.

We bought
cheap
gas station
lattes
and sat
on a curb
sipping them.
Well,
I sipped.
Brandt said
he didn't
like coffee.
Just wanted to
hold it
for the
warmth.

I thought
there was
a real
connection
between us.

Then suddenly,
Brandt got quiet.
I realized
he was
watching
a woman
cross the road.
She was older
and not dressed
sexy or
nothing like that.

I couldn't
figure what
about her
interested him.
But I knew
the look
in his
eyes
was . . .
          strange.

"I gotta go,"
he said.

And then
before I
could reply—

          he was gone.

I Got Grounded

for skipping school.

When Aunt Clara
told me,
I laughed right
in her face.

She didn't
have no
power
over me.

And I didn't
see any reason
to do anything
she told me
to do.

Like join
the snooty
film and photography club
at school.

They didn't just
have a darkroom.
They also had computers for
editing photos
plus a real nice
color printer.

Maybe I was
tempted.

A little.
I hadn't hardly
touched a camera
since that night
I found Mama's body.

Sometimes
my fingers would twitch
when I'd
see something
and know
exactly how I'd
frame it up.

But then, well then
it was like
it was too much.

I think partly
I was just too mad
at the world
to try and freeze
those little moments
that made it
beautiful.

I think partly
I wanted
to close my eyes
and let the world
spin on
without me.

Hot and Cold

That's how
it was
with Brandt.

One second,
I was sure
he liked me.
The next, he was distant.
Looking over my
shoulder
at a group
of college kids
headed to
the bar.
Again with
that funny look
that I couldn't
read.

Probably shoulda scared me.

Instead,
I was more
interested
than ever.

At school,
kids called him
a weirdo.

They whispered
about how he
mighta spent time
in jail or something
cause he missed
most of freshman year.

Whatever.
I didn't care
about their gossip.

I liked Brandt
a lot.

And I liked
that he
didn't seem to
belong nowhere.

Just like me.

It Became Clear

that I liked
Brandt
way more
than he
liked me.

He never
made a
move
to
kiss me.
Or even
hold my
hand.

Except
one time
when he
was
shivering
from the
cold,
and I said,

"Give me your hands."

Then I
held them
between
mine,

and blew
my warm
breath
onto him.

His eyes
got so
intense
then.
It sorta
freaked
me out.

"What?"
I asked.

"You,"
he answered.
"You're beautiful."

I lived
on those
words
for a
week.

But Then

Nothing
else like
that
happened.
I went back to
thinking
he wasn't
into me
at all.

But then
he'd say
something
like,

"What if
you could
live
forever?"

I shook my head.

"I'm barely
getting
through
right now.
Why would
I want
forever?"

It was
more
truthful
than I'd
meant
to be.

"I mean,
forever
is just
a long,
long
time."

Brandt nodded.

"Yeah, but
what if
we were
together
in forever?"

A jolt
of joy
struck
my
heart.

"What would
we do
with
forever?"

I asked,
leaning
into
Brandt.
Wondering
if he might
finally
kiss me.

Clueless,
he rolled away.
Leapt to his feet.
Spread his arms
out wide.

"We could
travel the
world.
Go anywhere
we wanted.
See everything
and take
our time,
because
we'd have
forever."

I squinted at him.
Wondering
if he was
pulling my leg.

But he
looked back
at me with
shining eyes.
And I knew
he meant it.

"Okay, sure,"
I said.

"Let's live
forever
and see
the world.

Why not?"

And Still He Didn't Kiss Me

Didn't make
any sorta
move.

If we were
just gonna
be friends,
that woulda
been okay.
But I was
sick of him
blowing
hot and cold.

So finally,
I just came
straight out
and asked,

"Do you
like me
or not?"

He seemed
surprised
by the
question.

"Course
I like
you."

I rolled
my eyes.

With boys
it's sometimes
hard to tell
when they're
being dumb
on purpose
or by
accident.

"I mean
LIKE,"
I said.

I put
my hand
to my
heart,
thumping it.

Brandt frowned
as if he were
offended.

"I knew
what you
meant,"
he said.

"And I
gave you
my answer."

For him
that was
the end
of that.

But I
was not
even a
little bit
satisfied.

"If you
like me,
then
kiss me."

It was a
challenge,
and Brandt
knew it.

Pucker up
or
shut up.

Standing,
he walked
away from me.

"I can't,"
he said.
"I want to,
but

I don't
trust
myself."

I rolled
my eyes,
"Don't worry,
I'll stop ya
before you
rip my
clothes off."

Brandt laughed,
bitter.
"That would
be the least
of it."

Good lord
almighty,
he was
the moodiest
most
dramatic
boy
in maybe
the entire
world.

If I
hadn't
fallen
so hard
for him,

I think
I mighta
hated him.

I decided
to give him
a taste
of his own
medicine.

"If you're
so dangerous,
then I'll
be going.
Bye!"

I gave him
my back
as I walked away.

Course he came
chasing after me.
His hot drawn
to my sudden cold.

But I was
all up in
my mad
by then.
I kept walking straight ahead
pretending
I didn't hear him
behind me,
asking me to stop.

We mighta gone
this way
till I made it
all the way
back to Clara's.
But then
a drunk
stumbled out of
a bar, and
decided to
get involved.

I didn't even
see the guy
until he
grabbed holda
my arm
and said,
"Hey there,
honey,
don't worry,
I got ya."

I guess
it didn't even
enter his
thick head
that maybe
I didn't want
to be gotten.
Not by him
or anyone else.

I grabbed at
his hair.
Pulling with
everything
I had.
I laughed
when he screeched,
high-pitched
and mad.

I'd been
in a fog
since Mama died.
Scared,
but also
        angry.

Furious really.

I had so much
mad,
I didn't know
where
to put it.

But just like
when I punched
Charity,
this guy was
giving it a place
to go.

Giving it my all,
I took a handful
of the man's hair
and yanked.

Which he
didn't like
one bit.

He let me know
with his fist.
It came 'round
so fast,
I didn't have time
to flinch.
It connected
with my spine.

I fell back
but he followed—
promising to
make me pay.

And then Brandt
was there.
He grabbed
the guy
like he was
nothing but a
small, yapping dog.
Picked him up
and gave him
a shake.

It made no sense.
The drunk was
a head taller
than Brandt
and thicker, too.
But Brandt
didn't even
seem to strain
as he shoved
the man
to the ground
and then
told him
with a cruel
smile,

"You don't even
know it,
but you're
already
dead."

I Coulda Sworn

Sharp teeth flashed
as Brandt smiled.

In that moment,
I honestly believed
he woulda bit
that man
if I hadn't grabbed
the back of
his shirt
and dragged him
away.

Course, the minute
we got away
further down the street,
my brain caught up
with me and I realized
how crazy that was.

Which is what
I said to Brandt.
"That was crazy."

He nodded
but looked distracted,
glancing over his shoulder
like he thought
that guy was
coming after us.

"Hey,"

I said,
trying to get
his attention.

"How didja
bring him down?
Was it like
some sorta
ninja kung fu or
what?"

At this
Brandt finally
looked at me.
Reaching out
his long fingers, he
touched the pulse
still beating hard
in my neck.

"You were scared,"
he said.

I swatted his hand away.
"Nuh-uh.
I was pissed.
I'm not
some
weak
little girl,"
I added.

"And that
dummy
back there
wasn't the
first man
to grab me."

I winced
where he'd punched
my spine.

"You're hurt,"
Brandt said.

"Yeah,
not the
first time
that's
happened
either."
I said,
with a
shrug.

Brandt
was silent
for a
moment,
then asked,
"What if
it was
the last?"

This actually
got a smile
outta me.
"You gonna
teach me
your kung fu?"

Brandt
grinned back.
"Something
like that."

Reaching
out for
my hand,
he said,
"I've got
a way
to make
you better
and
stronger
and just,
well,
            MORE."

It sounded
too good
to be true.
But I liked
the feel
of Brandt's
hand in
mine.

Even if
it was
ice-cold
as usual.

"I might
like that,"
I answered.
Then I leaned in.
Gave him
a kiss
on the
cheek.

To my
shock,
he pulled
me in.
Pressing
my body
against his.

I wondered
if he
could feel
the thump
of my
heart.

And if
his felt
the same.

Maybe
it did,
cause
when he
pulled away,
he said,
"I want
you
with me
forever,
just like
I said before."

He was
so over the top.
His eyes
burning
behind his
floppy hair.

"Okay,"
I said,
slightly
breathless.
Not even
sure what
I was
agreeing to.

It was
the right
answer
though.

Cause
Brandt
finally
pressed his
lips to mine.

It was
just a
peck
really,
but still
enough.

And even
better,
then he
added,
"I think
you should
come with me
and meet
some of
my friends."

"Who Lives Here?"

I asked.

"I do, kinda,"
Brandt answered.

"Nuh-uh,"
I said,
right away.
"This ain't
your house."

Brandt hated
talking 'bout it,
but he was a
rich boy.

Like really rich.

I figured this out
when he mentioned
all casual
how he didn't have
a car *no more*.

That the sweet SUV
he'd gotten for
his 16th birthday
wouldn't be returned
until he did everything
his dad said.
And Brandt
wasn't never
gonna do that.

Anyway,
this didn't look like
the type of house
someone who got
a brand new car
as a birthday gift
would live in.

This was the type
of house that
woulda better fit
my old life
with Mama.

This was the
type of place
you lived
when you didn't
have any
better options.

There were boarded-up
windows.
A yard overgrown
with weeds.

He shrugged
one shoulder.
"I guess technically,
my house is my dad's
big ugly brick colonial.
Or maybe it's my mom's
even bigger and uglier
modern monster
on the other side of town."

Brandt paused
and then studied
the house
like he was trying
to figure out
where it fit
in his life.

"But this,
            this is . . ."
He hesitated
once more.
Looked to me,
the house,
and then back
at me again.
"Maybe this isn't
a great idea."

There it was.
The hot
and cold
again.

I couldn't tell
whether he
was really
that mixed
up inside
or if he was
just messing
with me.

Either way
though,
we were here.
And the
angry, buzzing,
reckless feeling
that seemed
to live
in me
full time
was more alive
than ever.
It grew
in that
moment.
Till my skin
no longer
even seemed
to fit me
no more.

"I like bad ideas,"
I said.
Boldly,
I took Brandt's
hand in mine.
"And I
like you,
too."

Brandt squeezed
my hand.

"Sure, *now*,"
he said.
"But soon
you might
hate me."

"No. Never,"
I said,
believing it.

In that
moment,
I was
certain.
Brandt and I
would be
          together
                    forever.

It Was Dark Inside

The windows
that weren't
boarded up
were smeared
with grime.

It smelled
like rot.
Brandt said that was just
owing to the roof
leaking and the
constant damp.

But it
didn't smell
like damp.

It smelled
like death.

That shoulda
been the
first clue.

This place seemed
wrong.
But, at the same time—
familiar.
I felt weirdly
at home there—
in that dark room.

More than I
ever did
in Clara's
neat and tidy
house
that smelled
like lemons
or sometimes
roasted chicken.
It never ever smelled
like stale beer
and sweat
and vomit
like Mama's house.

Can you hate
something
and miss it
at the same time?

I guess so,
cause I did.

As We Came Down

the creaky old
staircase,
there were
two figures
standing
at the bottom.
Waiting for us.
And I knew
in a bone-deep
and certain sorta
way that
they were
the whole reason
Brandt had
brought
me here.

"Shelby,
this is
Sid and Tallie,"
Brandt said.

My First Impression

was of bones.

Sid and Tallie
looked
like skeletons
wearing thin
and worn-out
skin suits.

Their eyes were
huge in their
heads.
Empty of all
light.

Worst were
their teeth.
Yellow and
chipped.
Crooked.

They were like
the people in photos
I'd seen of survivors
of distant wars.
Where you
wondered
how they
were even
still alive.
I didn't like 'em
at first glance.

And as I got to
know 'em better,
I liked 'em
even less.

Sid was too quiet.
Tallie too loud.
Between the
two of them,
everything felt
                              off.

They were bad news.

But Brandt clearly
wanted me to
like them.

And them
to like me.

Or perhaps not
like
but approve.

As if
they were
his parents
instead of
two randos.

It seemed
I was being
presented
to them.

Like there
was some
sorta test
going on.

If it
weren't
for Brandt,
I woulda
told them
I didn't
want none of
what they
were selling.

But Brandt
was holding
my hand
again.
Saying,
"This is
Shelby,
and
I think
she's
the one."

I liked
being
the one.

I'd never
been
anyone's
"the one"
before.

I'd never
been
anyone's
anything
ever before.

With those
words,
Brandt
melted
the last
of my
walls.

I woulda
followed
him
to the ends
of the
earth.

The Girl

"So this is the girl
yer so
gone over,
huh?"
Tallie said,
with a smirk
at Brandt.

I glanced
at him.
Waiting
for him
to say
yes.

He just
shrugged.

"Well, she's
real pretty,"
Tallie said,
and then
reached out
to tug at
one of my curls.

"Look at this
purty hair.
Like a
cartoon
princess,
she is."

She turned to Sid.
He was silent
except for the click
of a piece of
hard candy
in his mouth.

"Ain't she a looker, Sid?"

He jerked his chin up
which I guess was
a yes.

Tallie cackled
and clapped her hands.
And then so sudden
I didn't even see
it coming,
she gripped my face
with one hand.
Fingers pressing
too tight
into the soft skin
above my jaw.

"All right,
pretty girl.
D'you
like Brandt
so much
you'd follow
him into
hell?"

I Thought of Mama

How she fell
for my daddy.
Kept falling further
and deeper,
until she
fell to pieces.

I looked toward Brandt,
who looked
like he was certain
I'd walk
            away.

My heart twisted.
He'd told me
I was the one.
He gave
that
to me.

And I wanted
to give him
that same feeling,
of being chosen
and
wanted,
above
            all
                    else.

I Turned

to Tallie
and the shadow
of Sid
behind her.

The smirk
was back
on her face.
Like she
already knew
my answer.

Lifting my
chin,
I told her,
"I'm with
Brandt.
Wherever
he goes."

Tallie Had a Laugh

that was
plain mean.

She cackled
at my
answer.
Said,
"There's
nothing
so dumb
as young
love."

I didn't like this.
It reminded me too much
of Grams.
Saying how
Mama loved
my Daddy
stupid.

But before
I could
think on that
further,
Tallie
linked
her arm
through mine.

Pulled me into
the dark sitting room.

"Alrighty,
then.
Might as
well make
it official
while your
feet are hot."

"Wait. Now?"
Brandt asked,
trailing behind us.

She ignored him.
Shoved me into
a threadbare chair.
She continued,
"Right then,
here it is
straight out.
We gotta
nice system
going on
with the
local junkies
round here.
See,
Sid and I got
unusual hungers.
And, junkies, well
they got hungers
of their own.
So tit for tat,
we help ones
like 'em
keep well satisfied.

Making sure they
get their high
nice
   and
       safe
          and
            clean.
Meanwhile they
give us
a little of what
we need
when we
need it."

I worried I'd
stumbled into
some sorta
human
trafficking
type of thing.

I looked
to Brandt.
Wanting
him to
tell me
it was
gonna be
okay.

"What is this?"
I asked.

Biting his lip,
he turned
to Tallie.

"Stop being
mean.
You know
she doesn't
understand,"
Brandt said.
"You gotta
show her,
and then
let her
        decide."

Tallie scoffed.
"Let her decide?
That part's
all done with.
She
    made
        her
            choice.
All that's left
now
is to
    make
        her."

"Make Me *What?*"

I asked.
                Anger
now mixing
with the fear.

My stomach twisted.
Cold spread all
up and down
my spine.

Tallie picked
up a bell sitting
on the table
beside her.
She rang it
ruthlessly.

Almost
immediately,
three junkies
came running in.

A woman,
maybe 20,
went right to Sid.
Rolled up the
sleeve on her
right arm.
Stuck it
under Sid's nose.
A slow smile
creased his face.

His smile was
an awful thing.
Sharp
        yellow
                teeth.
His eyes came alive
with something
that had not even
a tiny bit of
        pretty
                or good
                        or kind
in it.

Sid smiled ugly.
Evil.

And it scared me
straight down
to my
        toes.

I'd Seen Videos of Snakes

So still and unmoving
until a meal
presented
itself.
And then—
   they
     STRUCK.

Sid was like that.

His teeth—
   no, his
    fangs—
sank into
the crook
of the
junkie's arm.

The woman
jerked when
he struck
but then
went still
as he began
to . . .
    suck.

There was
nothing
else he
could've
been doing

other than
drinking the
blood straight
outta her.

I could see
his throat
working.
Swallowing.

His eyes
had closed.
The look on his face . . .

Well, I knew
that look.

I'd seen it
on Mama.

It was peace.
It was coming home
to the only place
where she'd
ever truly been happy.

It was getting
                high.

I'll Never Forget After

How Tallie laughed
with her
red-stained lips.
While blood
dripped
from her chin.
"You should
see the look on
yer face."

I'd been
so focused
on Sid.
I hadn't
even noticed
that she'd—

— That she'd
  — That she'd
    — That she'd —

I didn't know
what to name it.
The thing
Sid and Tallie
were doing.

Or I did
know,
but wanted
to play dumb.

Because
naming would
make it real.
And I wanted this
    to be
        a bad
            dream.

I'd already seen
enough in this
world
to know
it was full of
living nightmares.

And this
was surely
one of 'em.

In that dark room,
Sid and Tallie
drank
    fed
        feasted
on the blood
of another person.
Their teeth
like needles
finding the vein.
Taking instead of delivering.

For her and Sid,
the junkies were the drug,
and they were the addicts.

"Help."

I croaked
out the
word.
Or maybe
it was
a prayer.
A plea.

I stood and
my legs
wobbled
beneath me.
My head swam.

"Help,"
I said again.
This time looking to
Brandt. He stood,
coming toward me.
Arms outstretched.

I fell
into them.
And then
everything
went white
        before
                finally
                    falling
                        away.

I Dreamt

I was in the
darkroom at school,
carefully developing photos.

For some reason,
I couldn't
remember
what I'd
photographed.

And no matter
how I tried,
the pictures
remained
blank.

I must have
exposed
the film.
Ruining them,
turning what mighta
been beautiful
into a
       nothing—
             a blank.

Later, I Woke

An awful
metallic taste
in my mouth.

I was lying
on a bed.
My clothes
damp with
sweat.

For several
long moments,
I couldn't
recall
anything.

Not even
my own
        name.

I was
as blank
as the film
in my
dream.

But
too soon,
images
from the
previous
night

rushed in.
One after
another.
Overlapping
one horror
over the
next.

More than
anything,
I wanted
to be told
there'd been
a gas leak.
Or I'd been
poisoned—
          something,
                    anything,
to explain
                              away
what I'd seen.

My hand
lifted,
touching
my neck.
It came
away
          bloody.

I Stood Carefully

Afraid of
fainting
again.

But my legs
stayed solid
beneath me.

With my
hand pressed
to my neck,
I took a
few steps
to the mirror
over the
old dresser.

A gasp
escaped me
when I saw the
chunk of flesh
missing from
my neck.

My horrified
face
stared back
at me.
Ghostly pale.
Even my lips
had gone
white.

All the
blood that
should've
been coloring
my face
instead stained
the front of
my shirt.

And more blood
was still
coming out
of me.

How was
I still alive?

Or . . .
          maybe I wasn't.

"Wakey, Wakey."

The door
swung open.
Tallie barged in.

"Oh good,
yer up,"
she said and then
plunked
a mug down
on the dresser
in front of me.

"Here you are—
the drink of life,"
she said.
"Drink up."

The mug held
not coffee
or milk,
      but blood.

Red and thick.
Like a bottle of
cough syrup.
It shoulda
made me
      gag.

Instead,
my stomach
        growled
and my mouth
        watered.

Right then,
I coulda fought it.
Coulda thrown that mug
in Tallie's grinning face.

But I didn't.

Instead I clasped
the mug
with two hands
brought it to my lips
and drank it down
to the
        last
                d
              r
                o
                p.

I'm Not a Saint

I never
wanted
to be
like
Mama.
At the same time,
there was some . . .
                curiosity.

Which is to say,
there were
a few times
I flirted
with substance
abuse.

At seven,
I drank the
clear liquid
at the bottom
of a bottle.
Puked it all up.

At 10,
Mama's boyfriend Jakey
moved in for a bit.
He'd pass me
his vape pen
and I'd take it.

And last year,
there were
pills left
behind on the
kitchen table
after a party.

I was bored.
And lonely.
I took two.

Lost that day
and the next.
The days were just . . .
                    gone.

All those times,
I think what I really wanted
was to understand
what it was that Mama
loved so much.
Loved more than me.

Now though,
with a belly
full of blood,
I finally
got it.

Mama didn't
choose
the drug.
It chose her.
It owned her.

It called her
like them
sirens from
Greek myths.

It only took
one sip
to understand
everything.

I used to
belong
to myself.
But not anymore.

Now . . .
        the blood
                owned me.

The V Word

Brandt visited me
that first day
when I was
still reeling.
Right after Tallie
had given me
my first feeding.

After a cautious
tap at my door,
he came right in.
Sat at the end of
my bed,
where I was
already curled
up into a
miserable ball.

"They did it
to me, too,"
he said by way
of greeting.

"Why?"
I asked,
trying to understand.

"I wanted them to do it,"
he said.
Both a smile and sneer
twisted his lips.

"Practically
begged them.
About a year
and a half ago,
my father hit me.
Knocked a tooth
right outta my head."

He paused.
"That's when
I decided
that I'd had
enough of it.
I wanted
to be
stronger.
I wanted
to be
bigger.
Better
than he
could
ever be."

I nodded.
I understood this.

"How'd you
know about them?
Sid and Tallie.
And what
they are . . ."

"My cousin, Finn,
was into drugs.
He found
Sid and Tallie—"

I interrupted,
"What are they
anyway?
The only thing
I keep thinking
is—"

Brandt's hand
covered my mouth.
Gently.
Leaning in,
he warned,
"Never use
the V word.
Something
about it
triggers Sid.
He goes
plain crazy.
Tearing up and into
anything
in his way."

I don't doubt
that Sid is capable
of destruction
and terror.

"Don't try
any Transylvanian
accents, either."

Leaning in
even closer,
he whispered,
"I vant to dreenk
your blud."

I giggled.
Surprised
to hear
the sound
come out of
me.

That I could
laugh at this
seemed so wrong.
And yet also . . .
it was a relief.

"Okay,"
I answered,
my lips
brushing against
the inside of
his palm.

Air gusted out
of him.
Brandt's fingers
stroked my cheek
before he pulled
his hand away.

"You're warm,"
he observed.

"It's always
that way after
you drink.
It warms
you from
the inside out.
Then you
start going cold.
Then colder still
with every hour
that passes."

"And then?"
I whispered the question.

Again that twist of his lips.
"Then you drink again."

He stood.
I was tempted
to pull at his hand.
Instead, I asked,
"But then what are we?"

Brandt sighed.

"We're immortal.
We're strong.
We need blood."

So far, none of that
sounded too bad.

"What about daylight?
Will it burn us?"

I asked.

"Nah," Brandt said,
"it's just sorta hard on
your eyes sometimes."

"So what's the downside?"
I asked.

Brandt frowned.
"The hunger.
You don't know,
not yet, but you will.
From now on, you don't
belong anywhere—except here."

I didn't understand.

"You'll see,"
Brandt said.

"You'll see, and then
you'll wish I'd never
brought
          you
                    here."

And with that
he left.

Over the Next Few Days

I was like
a baby
again.

I slept mostly.
Woke only to drink
the blood Tallie
brought me.

When my mouth
was dry, it wasn't
water I wanted.

When my belly
rumbled, it wasn't
food I craved.

The world shrank
to that tiny room.

And my only joy
was in my daily
mug.

I might have
lived that way
forever,
but one day
as I was licking
the last drops
of blood
from my cup,

Tallie announced,
"Enjoy it, luv.
After this,
you get yer own."

I jerked my head up,
surprised.
"Huh?"

Tallie grinned, mean.
"Didja think I'd be
waiting on ya,
the rest of our
endless lives?"

I blinked at her.
Then down at
my empty mug.
"But how . . .?"

She laughed, hard.
"Yer fangs
have come in
by now.
So you just
pick a warm body
and ask 'em
to let ya have
a bite."

Blood was
dark under
my fingernails.

From where I'd
run my fingers
round the
edges of my cup.

But still,
I jerked back
at those words.
At the thought
of sinking my teeth
and biting through
the flesh
of another
          person.

It's the difference
between
getting a burger
at the drive-thru
and having to
go out and
butcher yer
own cow.

"I can't do it,"
I told Tallie.

"Well then,"
she replied,
plucking the mug
from my hands.
"You'll starve."

It Was No Ordinary Hunger

And I
began
to understand
Brandt's
warning.

I lasted less than
one full day
before I was
begging Tallie
for one more mug.
Tears in
my eyes.

She took real pleasure
in telling me
                no.

"You did this to me.
You have to feed me!"

Which, of course,
only made Tallie
laugh again.
"Nuh-uh, luvie.
You were made
cause you
were wanting
to be more
than you were."

Again that
awful laugh
rattled outta her.
She added,
"Next time,
be more
careful whatcha
wish for."

One of the Blood Givers

eventually
took pity on me.
Showed me how
Tallie had used
a needle with a
tube at the end
to get their blood
out without
using any teeth.

Being users,
they had no trouble
sticking themselves.
For one day,
I drank outta my mug
again.

But Tallie
got wind of it.
Nipped that
right in the bud.

Grabbing me
by the back
of the neck,
she hauled me
to a mirror
and lifted up
my front lip.

"Look there,"
she said.

"See those
pointy things?
Those are yer fangs.
They ain't just
for show."

I jerked away
from her.
Angry.
Knowing
she got off on
watching me
twist and spin.

"Maybe I just won't drink
no more blood,"
I said to her.
I knew it for a lie
even as the words
were on my lips.

Tallie knew it, too.
Laughed so hard
she had to
bend over and
clutch her sides.

Then she grabbed
me once again.
Hauled me to
the front door.
And without
even a goodbye
or good luck—
tossed me out.

It'd Been Days

since I'd entered
that house.
The sudden rush
of fresh air
reminded me
the rest of
the world
still existed.

Including Aunt Clara.

She'd left me
a million or so
frantic text messages.
I'd ignored 'em
until she threatened
to call the police.

I'm not much
of a fan
of law enforcement.

And I had a feeling
Sid and Tallie
wouldn't thank me
for bringing 'em
to their door neither.

So I'd texted her back
and told her
I was safe.
That I'd be gone
for a while.

I'd wanted
to get away
from Clara's
from the moment
I'd gotten there.

And yet,
at that moment
the thought
of my clean bed
in the pretty
blue guest room
at Aunt Clara's
made me feel
something like
                longing.

Except how could
I go back there
or anywhere else
like this?

With the taste of
blood
on my tongue,
and yet still
    thirsty
        for
            more.

Brandt Found Me

sitting on
a broken-down
lawn chair
that'd been
left to rot
in the yard.

He seemed relieved
to see me.

"I thought
you'd gone,"
he said.

"Where would
I go?" I asked.
Hoping he might
have an answer.

"I shouldn't have
brought you here,"
he sighed.

For the first
time, I found
his sad boy act
annoying.

"Well, you did,"
I snapped at him.

"So stop telling me
how yer
sorry about
how things
happened.
And tell me what
I'm meant
to do next!"

The words came out
vicious enough
that he took a
quick step away.

"Easy,"
he cautioned.
"Being hungry
is already
gonna bring
out your worst.
Even Sid
can't always
control it."

Brandt pointed to my neck.

"Tallie had him
do the honors—
that's what she
called it.
But once he had
his teeth in you,
he didn't want to
stop."

I felt sick,
imagining Sid's
fangs and lips
on the soft skin
of my neck.

"She yelled at him,
yanked his hair,
and then finally
broke a chair
in half.
Clubbed him
in the back
of the head."

I turned my back
to Brandt,
hating him
a little bit
for telling me.
For putting
ugly pictures
in my head.

Staring at the
crumbling
brick wall,
I could finally
ask
the one question
that had been
sitting unsaid
between us.

"Am I dead?"

Brandt sighed.
"Tallie says
we're not
chained with
the living
or the dead.
We're
                between."

Between.
This strangely
felt exactly
                right.

And also
oh-so
                wrong.

I was less than alive.
But not quite dead.

With that,
I had only
one more
question
for Brandt.

"Why me?"
I asked him.

At this, he
looked surprised.
Like the answer
was obvious.

"I liked
you.
And . . .
I was lonely.
And you had nothing else
going on
in your life.
You seemed like
maybe . . .
you wouldn't mind."

I Understood Brandt

and his hot/cold
ways, at last.

He'd been wrestling
with himself.
Wanting company
in his misery.
I guess I proved that
I was the right
type of idiot to walk right
into Sid and Tallie's
arms . . .
or should I say
fangs?

I think a part
of me had been
hoping for some
sorta declaration
of love.
Maybe him going on 'bout
how he couldn't
live without me.

Or *unlive*
without me.
But now
thinking
on it,
I can
see that

Brandt
never promised me love.

Only . . .
        forever.

I Hated Him a Bit

But I needed
Brandt, too.

He was the one
who told me
it wasn't
a good idea
for me to
go back to
Aunt Clara.
Especially
while I was
hungry.

He also showed me
that there were
ways around
the whole
blood problem.

We took a trip to
the grocery store.
He taught me how
sinking our fangs
into a raw steak
could blunt
the edge
of hunger.

The red meat
was gray
when we
finished with it.

That night,
he got the keys
to Sid and Tallie's
old Caddy.
I slept in
the back seat.

The next day,
I convinced
Brandt
that we should
take it
for a drive.

It started hard,
but once it got
going, it wasn't
too bad of a ride.

Without school
or anything else
to fill our days,
we began
bumping along
country roads
pockmarked with
potholes.

We ran the heat.
Pressed our
hands to the vents
fighting off the cold
inside of us.

A week went by.
Then half of
another.

We ran
low on money.
Had to steal
the meat.
Stuffing the
cellophane-wrapped
packages under
our shirts.
Running outta
the store when
a manager
asked us
what we were doing.

It was just
as well
we couldn't
go back after that.
I was racked with
shivers by then.
The blood in the meat
not enough to ever
fully warm me
or stop the
cravings.
They grew
fiercer with each
passing day.

"I can't bite someone,"
I told Brandt.

He nodded
in response,
but his words
disagreed.
"You could.
It's not the biting
that's hard.
It's the stopping."

I asked then
if that had
happened to him.
If he'd used
his fangs
on a person . . .
        If he'd killed.

Instead of answering,
he pulled the car
to the side
of the road.
Then he walked
away,
        leaving me
                alone.
When he came back,
we didn't talk
about it no more.

But I was pretty
certain his reaction
meant the answer
            was
                yes.

Passing the Time

became a problem.

Brandt started
talking 'bout
how we
oughta
travel
and go
places.

But to me,
it seemed
like wherever
we went,
it'd
always be
just him
and me.

Most of the time
we were bored
and sick of
each other's company.

We still ate food
and drank water,
but nothing
tasted good
except blood.

The idea that we'd
live forever,
with only
one another,
felt
not
like
a gift,
but more like
        a curse.

I Started Taking Photos

with Brandt's phone.
It was a whole heckofalot
nicer than mine.

I took close-ups
of my fangs.

Or of Brandt's
mouth with a ribeye
clamped between
his teeth.

Careful
not to give our
identities away.
I broke us up
into bits and pieces.

Mr. Bailey
used to say
that an artist
ain't really an artist
until they
send their work
out into the
world.

So I made an
InstaPic account.
I called it
The Art of Being a Vampire.

Over the next
few weeks,
I gained a couple
thousand followers
who were
interested enough
to comment.
They'd ask questions
        (that were no doubt
        meant as a joke)
about my
bloodsucker life.

I was so
hungry
that sometimes
I'd sink
my fangs
into my own hand.
Just to trick
my body into thinking
        (for a few seconds anyway)
that it was being fed.

But when
I was
framing up
my subject
and deciding
on the light
and angles,
for those
few minutes
the hunger faded.

And
for that
short time, I felt
  <<<almost>>>
    human.

We Ran Outta Money

And so we had
no choice
but to start
stealing
more than
just steaks
from the
grocery store.

At first,
it was
fun.

We'd get
ourselves
blooded up.
Then,
feeling like
we were
unstoppable,
we broke
windows
to a
jewelry store.
Sold the goods
to a
pawn shop.

The money
bought us
gas
and

blood soup
from this
weird
Polish
restaurant.

After that,
we set
our sights
on a
bigger
target.

A blood drive
at the
local Y.

I was meant to
cause a
distraction
while Brandt
got the goods.

"Just scream
and pretend
you're sick
or something,"
he'd told me.

So that's what
I did.

Sick wasn't
hard to fake—

my cheeks
were hollow.
My skin
a sickly,
chalky
white-gray
sorta color.

I avoided
my reflection.
Fearing
I was
beginning
to look like
Sid and Tallie.

"Oooh,"
I moaned,
soft at first.
"I don't feel good."

This was true.

The moment
I'd walked in,
the smell
of blood
turned me
more
animal
than
person.

The people
in that

room
mighta been
wrapped up
in cellophane
just like
the steak
at the
grocery store,
cause that's
how I
saw 'em—
          as meat.

It was
all I
could do
to keep
from
grabbing
the nearest
warm body.
Sinking
my fangs
into 'em.

Somehow,
I resisted.

Recalling
the plan,
I went back
to being sickly.

"AUUUGH,"
I yelled.

A few heads
turned my
way.
Concern
on their faces.

But I needed
more than
that.

Clutching my head,
I headed for
a table
stacked with
brochures.

Pretending
to trip,
I tumbled
into them.
Sent papers
flying.
Threw myself
onto the floor.

Almost immediately
people began
to gather 'round me.

"You okay, hun?"
a woman asked,
touching my arm.

She was so close
I could smell her
soap.
Beneath it,
the meat of her body.
Like tenderloin.
     But better—
         fresher—

And I coulda sworn
my ears were
picking up
the thump of
her heart.
The slosh
of her blood
as it flowed
through her body.

I imagined
her veins
and the blood
in 'em.
Like a river.
All I needed
to do
was dip
a hand in—

"Hun?"
she asked again
as I clapped
a hand over
my mouth.

Feeling my fangs
pushing against
my upper lip,
wanting out.

"She's gonna
be sick,"
someone else said.
Several people
stepped back a little.

That gave me
space enough
to escape.
I got to
my feet.
I shot through
the crowd
and then out
the door.

I ran and ran
with everything
I had left.
Finally,
I could go
no further.

Feet heavy,
I stumbled
into an area
of heavy brush
and collapsed.

Brandt Found Me

Put a piece of meat
to my lips.
The way
you would
a cup of
water for
someone who'd
just come outta
the desert.

"How'd you find me?"
I croaked.

"I'm connected
to you,
cause I
made you,"
he answered.

I frowned at this.

"But Sid bit me,
                right?"
Something flickered
across Brandt's face
but was gone
before I could
name it.

"Yeah,"
he said, at last.

"But I brought you
to them."

There was something
missing in that
answer.
I mighta asked
more questions
except that I
noticed the flush
in Brandt's face
and the warmth
coming from
his body.

"You fed,"
I said, the words
coming out
like an
accusation.

He went
even pinker.
His eyes
flicked away
from mine.

"There was a guard,"
he said,
his voice low.
"He caught me
at the door."

Brandt swallowed hard,
before continuing.

"I let him
pull me into this
back room,
and then . . ."

He stopped there.
Clearly
not wanting
to say the rest.

But I needed
to know
the worst
of it.

"Is he . . .
　　　　　　dead?"

Brandt was
silent for so long,
I thought he
wouldn't answer
at all.

But finally,
he said,
"I drained him.
Not just for me,
but for you.
We can't keep
surviving on
sucking the
juices outta
T-bone steaks."

My eyes
sank closed.
"What about
the blood
donation?"
I asked.

"I lost those,"
Brandt said.
"I'm sorry."

I laughed
and the sound
was bitter . . .
and it made me
think of Tallie
again.

"Well what
am I
supposed
to do now?"
I asked him.

Brandt pointed
to his neck.
"Use your teeth.
You have to
bite someone
sooner or later.
At least
I'm willing."

I'd Once Wanted

to kiss Brandt
in the pouring rain.

That seemed like
a long, long,
          looooong
time ago.

Since turning
into this,
all thoughts
of romance
with Brandt—
          or anyone else—
had
disappeared.

My hunger
filled me up.
There wasn't
space for
nothing else.

When I looked
at Brandt,
I'd stopped
wondering
about how
his lips would
feel pressed
against mine.

All I saw
in him
and every other
living thing
was the blood
beneath their skin.

I pressed
my fingers
to Brandt's neck,
feeling the
big artery there.
Swollen thick
like a stream
turned into
a raging river
after a long
rainfall.

He was fat
as a tick
on that
security guard's
blood.
And instead
of making
me sick,
all I felt
in that moment
was the desire
to get
my share
of what'd
been taken.

I leaned into
Brandt.
All my past
hesitation
forgotten.

"Wait,"
he said.

He put one
of his hands
round my neck,
then squeezed
hard enough
I could feel
the pressure
on my windpipe.

"Gotta have
a way
to cut
you off,"
he explained.
"Otherwise,
you'll drink me
dry."

I wanted to
tell him
that would
never happen.

But I was
almost woozy
with hunger.

And the part
of my brain
that said
Thou Shalt Not
        (always in Grams's voice)
had gone
silent.

"Sure,"
I said.
Then I
pressed my
lips
to Brandt's
neck.

I tasted salt
and something
else that was
uniquely him.
Then my fangs
pierced his skin.
Blood
filled my
mouth,
    drowning
        out
            everything
                else.

I Gulped the Blood

Barely noticed
when his
grip round
my neck
grew tighter.
When the sound
of his blood—
now my own—
roared in my
ears.

Even as
my throat
closed,
stopping
air and
blood
from getting
through,
I continued
to suck.
          Wanting MORE.
Until at last,
     it all went
          black.

The Photos I Took

of the
black and blue
bruises round my neck
in the
shape of
Brandt's
fingers
were
strangely
beautiful.

Or at least
I thought so.

But the comments
I got
were no
longer
fun.

"Hun,
this is
abuse,"
one said.

And others
agreed.

"Your man
is no good
for you,"
another wrote.

To my
surprise,
I answered,
"I know."

I called that
photo
     Loved Him Stupid.

Brandt and Me

made the news
that night.

Turns out
Y's
are full of
cameras.
They'd
gotten good
pictures of
Brandt's face.

Plus,
since
Brandt and I
had walked in
together,
it was possible
someone there could
give a description of me.

Which is
to say,
it turns out
Brandt and I
were a pair
of dummies.

"Sid and Tallie
will kill me.
They told me so.

Said to do what
I wanted
but keep it
quiet."

Brandt clenched
his phone
tight in his hand
as he told
me this.

The blood drive
incident was the
top story
on the local
news station app.
It seemed
that Brandt
was
at large.
Considered
dangerous.

This was
pretty much
the opposite of
quiet.

"What now?"
I asked.

Brandt stared up
at the sky
like it might
have an answer
for him.

Maybe it did,
cause a
moment later
he said,
"We gotta run,
of course."

He said it like
it was the
obvious answer.
Which I
suppose it was.

Still, I didn't like
him thinking
that I'd
come along
no questions asked.

Cause I had questions.
Lots of 'em.
And they were
getting asked.

Starting with,
"Wait a minute.
You said you
could find me
cause you made me.

Won't Sid and Tallie
find *you*
the same way?"

Brandt sighed heavy,
like I tuckered him out.

He'd been doing that
a lot lately.
Often with a promise
to tell me whatever
I wanted to know
                              later.

A later that never came.
But not this time.

"Just tell me,"
I demanded.

So he did.

He told me
how his junkie
cousin, Finn,
who brought
him to
Sid and Tallie's
was also
the one who
made him.

"Where is Finn now?"
I asked.

"Does it matter?"
Brandt asked.

When I
nodded yes,
he sighed again.

"He's dead.
Okay?"
Then he stomped away.

There was something
in the way
he'd said it.
Some hesitation.
It made me wonder.

I had Brandt's phone
cause I'd been
taking photos earlier.
It was an easy thing
to open Brandt's
Facelook app.
Scroll through
his contacts
looking for a Finn.

I found him quick.

He was maybe
25
and very much
alive—
with a wife
and
a new little baby.

So Brandt Was a Liar

Just how big of one, I didn't know yet.

Finn wasn't dead.

Was he ever even a vampire
in the first place?

And if he was…
then did he turn back
again?

Brandt had always claimed
to feel
                    bad
about
changing me.

He acted
like he was
full of
                    regrets.

And maybe
he was.

But what if there was a
larger truth?

What if
Brandt had known
all the while

I could be
      turned
            back?

Maybe he knew,
but made
sure that
    I
           didn't.

The thought
made me feel sick.

Brandt Returned

Full of ideas
'bout how we
oughta go to
Alaska,
cause he'd
always wanted
to see it.

I asked what
the heck was
in Alaska.
He told me
moose.

Which made
me laugh
and made him
                mad.

Not that I cared.

"We ain't going
nowhere till we
get some money,"
I told Brandt.

I tossed
his phone at him.
Added,
"Maybe your
cousin would
let us borrow
some."

Brandt didn't
have enough
blood in him
to blush.
And maybe
he wouldn't
have anyhow.

He seemed
more angry
than ashamed
at being caught
in a lie.

"You wanna
know the truth?"
he snapped at me.
"After turning me,
Finn got cold feet.
Went to
my father—
told him it was
drugs.
Asked him
to send us both
to rehab."

"Did he?"
I asked.

Brandt nodded,
a short jerk
of his head.

"He sent us.
I ran away
the second day.
Finn stayed.
Got clean,
or whatever."

He turned away
like that was that.
End of story.

But it wasn't,
          not for me.

"What's clean
or whatever?
You mean he's
not a bloodsucker
no more?
You mean
we can go back
to being
          normal?"

I figured
this was
exactly
what it meant,
but I wanted
Brandt to admit it.

At this, Brandt
spun and
came at me,

a dangerous
light in
his eyes.

"It takes going through hell
to get back
to the living.
And—
you wanted this,"
he added.
"You hated your life.
You told me
you 'wouldn't
never come to
nothing.'
Those were
your words
exactly.
In that
hillbilly way
you talk.
So don't pretend
like you
didn't
say it."

I nodded.
"I said it,"
I agreed,
my voice cold.
Brandt sniffed,
like he'd been
proven right.

"Yeah. So.
There ya go.
That's why I bit ya."

I stared at him.
I heard his words
and knew he'd let slip
something
that I wasn't
meant to know.

"*You* bit me.
          Not
                    Sid."

I wanted it
          to be
                    real clear.

"What's it matter?"
Brandt asked,
turning away.

"It matters,
cause you
told me
a story
'bout Sid.
But now I think
it was
                    YOU
had to be
hit over the head
to keep from
bleeding me dry."

I yelled the words
at his back.

Brandt whirled round
once more,
coming back at me.

"You don't wanna
go to Alaska?
Fine.
I'm leaving
in the morning.
With or
without you."

I imagined this life
in Alaska.
Forever
with Brandt (and moose).

I imagined us
roaming the world
trying to
outrace
our hunger.
And failing.
    Again
        and
            again
                and
                    again.

And then I knew
what I had to do.

The Only Way to Set Brandt Free

While he
was asleep,
I put
my fangs
into
his neck.
In the
same spot
as before.

But this
time,
he wasn't
holding
me back.

He woke,
while I
drank.
And his
eyes
stared at
me.

I expected
him
to struggle.
But instead,
he sorta
smiled.

"Knew
        you . . .
                were—
                        the one."

Those were his
last words.

And Then Brandt Died

And I kept
   on
      drinking
till he
was empty.

I carried
his body,
so light—just bones.
Left him at the
back door
to Sid and Tallie's.

I knew Sid and Tallie
would be asleep now.

I saw a junkie in the window.
Held up a lighter.
Mouthed, "Get the others out, now."
She listened,
and three of the others
ran out of the door, too.

Maybe toward
some new start.

Maybe no one
is too far gone
long as they still got
some life in 'em.

Let It Burn

Then I
poured
lighter fluid
I'd shoplifted
from the
minimart.
Set Brandt's bones
and
that ugly
wicked house
on fire.

I took
a picture
of the house
as the
flames
stretched
   toward
     the
       early
         morning
           sky.

I called it:

(Two Wrongs) Trying to Make It Right.

I Considered

walking into
the flames
myself.
But I couldn't
make myself
do it.

Maybe I just knew
I wasn't too far gone.
There was some part of me
worth saving.
Maybe,
just maybe,
there was
still
something good
I was
       meant
          to do.

Brandt's Cousin, Finn

had given
me an idea.
And it grew
into a
thought.
And that thought
wouldn't
go away.

For the first time
in a long time,
all I really wanted
was to be
                alive.

I Broke into Aunt Clara's

Well, I used
my key.

I was relieved
it still worked.
She hadn't
changed the locks
on me.
Not even after everything.

I'd made sure
to wait
until after
I'd seen
Aunt Clara
leave for work.
So the place
was empty.

Everything
in the room
Clara had
given me
was the same
as I'd left it.

Quickly,
I packed
clothes
into a bag.

Then I reached
under the bed
for the box
with Mama's
ashes.

It'd been
her wish
to have 'em
spread
somewhere pretty.

I'd been
too mad
at her
to do it before.
But now
I was at last
ready to
lay Mama
to rest.

After all I'd
been through,
all my
cravings,
I understood
her in some
sorta way.

She'd done
the best
she could
by me.

And even if
it wasn't
enough,
well,
it was
better than
        nothing.

The Photo Was There, Too

The one
I'd called
    Fear the Future.

At the time,
I'd meant it
to be some
sorta warning
to Mama's
younger self.
But I know
I was
mostly
thinking
of myself.

Of my
        future.

Of my
        fear.

But I
didn't
fear the future.
Or not that
much.
Not anymore.

I'd already hit
the deepest
rock bottom,
where there
was almost
no light
to be found.

But maybe
cause of
all those
years of
photography,
I'd gotten
good at
finding
the light.

Now like
the aperture
on my camera,
I just hadta
open myself up
and let
            all that
                    light
                        get in.

Hope Was Odd

The sorta feeling
that I worried
would go away
just as quick
as the bubbles
in a glass
of soda.

Maybe that's
why I moved
quick.
Wanting
to finish
the plan
while I was
still fizzin'
with faith
and hope
and courage.

I Called Aunt Clara

"I'm home."

The word
felt strange
in my
mouth.

But Grams
always said
to begin
as you mean
to go on.

On her end
of the phone,
Aunt Clara
started
to cry.

Which
at first
I thought
was her
upset
that I was
in her house.

But then
she said,

"Thank God.
I thought
you were
        dead."

And she
cried
even harder.

When she
got herself
under control,
she told me
she was
already
on her
way
home.
She asked me
        please
to wait
for her.

Somehow,
that *please*
almost
undid me.

I Stayed

Even though it
was hard.
I nearly
walked out
more than
once
only to
turn back
again.

Finally,
she came
rushing in.
Tears still
running
down her
face.

She wanted
to hug me.
But I put a
hand out,
stopping her.

"I can't,"
I said.
"I'm all
messed up."

To my shock,
she nodded.

Like she
understood.

"What can
I do?"
she said.
"How can
I help?"

This then
was the
    true
        test.

Was I my
bad blood?

Was I
doomed
to be
my mama?

Or could I
imagine
myself
in a picture
where I
was not
broken up
into pieces?

Could I see
myself as

                whole?

"I Wanna Go to Rehab."

I heard
myself
say the
words.

It didn't
feel real.

Or like
enough.

So I
said 'em
again.
Aunt Clara
was already
nodding
her head.

That's when I
fell to
my knees
and at last
let myself
cry.

Nobody Believed

I was a
V-word
or that
I was addicted
to blood.

They thought
the fangs
were some
kinda
tooth decay.

And that
my need
to be away
from people
was shame
or something
like that.

I didn't
tell 'em
they were wrong.

Sometimes,
I even thought
that maybe
I was just
a junkie
like Mama.

And all
the rest
of it
was just me
trying to
be something
special.

Eventually,
after weeks of
withdrawal—
and the kinda torture
that Grams always
said was meant
to be saved for those
that burn in hell—
my fangs started
to go away.

Forever was over,
which left me
hanging on
from minute to minute.
But I kept
letting the
light in.
And I kept on
believing
the pain was
worth it.
And I kept on
believing
I was
worth it.

But Even Then

I'd catch
the scent
of blood.
Or see
the blue veins
in someone's
wrist.
And the
hunger
would
  rise
    once
      more.

That's when
I knew.

Some of
the dark
would always
be with me.

I Fought Through It

with
the help of
Aunt Clara.

And oddly,
Brandt's cousin,
Finn.

I wrote
him a letter
from rehab.
Just saying
I was
a friend
of Brandt's.
Trying to get clean.
And to
my surprise,
he came
to visit me.

I told him
everything.
My full
confession.

His face went
all wrong
when I told
him how
I'd ended
Brandt.

But he
didn't hate me
for it.

Instead,
he said
I did
what he
couldn't.

That all I'd done
was end Brandt's curse.
And save so many lives.

And then
he asked for me
to
   forgive
      him.

I almost laughed.
No one had ever
asked me that before.

I guess life
could
sometimes
be funny
in a
haha way
that
wasn't
just plain mean.

I Started Using the Fancy Camera

from Aunt Clara.

Instead of
visiting
a darkroom,
I took
digital photos.
Learned
how to edit
them on a
computer, too.

It was different,
but even so,
there was
still
the same
old magic
in it.

And I was
better at it,
too.

I didn't
focus
on just
the ugly
or just
the
beautiful.

I found a
        middle ground.

And I
stopped
making
my camera
lens
a wall
between
me and
the rest of
the world.
Instead it was
    a bridge,
        a connection,
            to the
                human experience.

With every
click of
the shutter,
I now try
    to reach
        your heart.

And
at the
same time,
to give up
    a piece
        of
            my own.

That you
might
hold it.

That you
might
know it,
and
in doing so
see what
I see,
which is—
me in you
and
you in me.
And
all of us
just trying to
make it over
        around
                and
                        through
to that
   bright
      dawn
         light
that only comes
   after the
      darkest
         of nights.

WANT TO KEEP READING?

If you liked this book, check out another
book from West 44 Books:

THE REAL UNREAL
BY RYAN WOLF

ISBN: **9781978596689**

Bright
   spirals
     screaming.

NEW WORLD ORDER SCUM
shouts across
the brick
in a sharp yellow.

FREEDOM WINS
waves beside it,
a proud blue.

WE WILL NOT OBEY
has a
grim green grin.

And
in the bloodiest
drips
of hot red,
it reads:

> **ALL**
> **YOU**
> **DEVILS**
> **WILL BE**
> **JUDGED**

The graffiti
        is flung
everywhere.

Spat
on each side
of the building.
Sneering from
the limestone walls.

Bits of
broken glass
litter
the ground.
Sprinkled
        over
the sidewalk
like shiny
balls of hail.

What is left
of the windows
looks like
a thousand
tiny
teeth.

There are small gleams
of color
among the shards.

The stained glass
was over
a hundred years old.

But
what
does
it
matter?

Whoever did this
didn't care.

The vandals even
knocked
the nose
     off
one of the
gargoyles.

I don't know how
they reached
that high.

"NATE!"

For a moment
I imagine
the call comes
from the noseless gargoyle.

SEQUEL TO
not Hungry.

Always
JUNE

KATE KARYUS QUINN

CONTROL
ROOM

RYAN WOLF

THE
DRAGONS
CLUB

GYN BERMUDEZ

THE
BEST
PART IS
AT THE
END

CHECK OUT MORE BOOKS AT:
www.west44books.com

An imprint of Enslow Publishing

WEST **44** BOOKS™

About the Author

Kate Karyus Quinn is an avid reader and menthol chapstick addict. She lives in the suburbs of Buffalo, New York, with her husband, three children, and two dogs. She is the author of many books, including: several young adult books with HarperTeen, *Anti/Hero*, a middle grade graphic novel with DC comics, and *Not Hungry*, a book in verse that was a Junior Library Guild selection.

Find her online at www.katekaryusquinn.com or on Twitter and Instagram @katekaryusquinn.